SWOLE: LEG DAY

Published and written by: Golden Czermak
2nd Edition

WARNING: This is a **short story** written for mature readers. It is pure escapism, containing adult themes, coarse language, erotic sexual situations, male-male sex, and nudity.

This is a work of fiction. All characters, organizations, and events portrayed in this novel are products of the author's imagination and/or used fictitiously. All Rights Reserved.

In accordance with the United States Copyright Act of 1976, the scanning, uploading, or sharing of any part of this work without the permission of the copyright holder is unlawful theft of the author's intellectual property.

ACKNOWLEDGEMENTS

This work would not be possible without such great support from readers and others in the book community.

Special thanks to all my tree-trunk legged gym bros for inspiring this part of the erotic short story series. Squats for the win. #ThirdLeg

SWOLE
LEG DAY

CHAPTER 1

AFTER CHEST DAY

THE HANDLE ON THE FRONT door of a modern, hillside home jostled. Behind it was the sound of frustrated grunts and whispers.

"One more fucking thing to replace in this joint..." said a muffled voice, the man who owned it unmistakably aggravated. There was another rattle and the low *thump* of a shoulder against the wood. "Damn latch has started sticking again; it does this every time the weather ..."

He didn't get to finish the sentence, the door unexpectedly opening as it flung toward the wall. A quick and calloused hand grabbed it just before it struck. It was attached to a muscular arm that, in turn, hung out of a wrinkly sleeveless tee.

"That was close," he said, giving his thick beard a good scouring with his fingertips. Adjusting a gym bag that hung off his broad shoulder, the man swaggered into the dark foyer.

"No kidding, Trent," said a shorter, thinner silhouette as it followed, closing the unruly door behind them. "That dent would have been yet another thing for you to repair."

"Yeah, yeah Jonny-boy, point out the obvious," Trent replied, smirking as he turned to see Jonny standing there all innocent and cute. He knew that appearance was deceiving. Looking up to the ceiling, Trent pointed and said, "I was thinking more about waking the sleeping beast that is Jared Hughes. Frankly, I don't want to deal with any of his bullshit right now."

Bullshit? Jonny wondered, his face squashed together as if he'd bitten a large chunk out of a lemon. *From Jared? What'd he mean by that?*

There was obviously some water under the bridge, but before Jonny could ask Trent was talking again.

"Besides," he continued, emerald eyes locked back on Jonny, "I don't think you'd mind seeing me work hard… *again*."

With that said, Trent's smirk became a lip bite and he reached down to the ends of his tee, stripping it off. As the fabric rolled over the tight curves and deep lines of his upper body, they seemed to gleam with a light of their own.

Jonny's eyes widened, and his asshole twitched, thinking of the time the two spent entangled with and inside each other last night – or rather that morning – at Trent's gym. Jonny realized that it was aptly named Swole and not just for the muscles that got a good pump within its walls.

"Jesus that needs to be washed," Trent said of the shirt, casually dropping it to the floor. "Oops."

Jonny snapped back from his rambling thoughts as Trent then slowly, and downright deliberately, bent over to pick it up.

"Y-you're right, I w-wouldn't mind t-that at all," he stammered, rubbing lightly on his sore chest. "By the way, that was a great workout last night. I'm feeling it for sure."

"Already? Mission accomplished then," Trent said proudly. "I suspect you're going to be feeling a lot of things this week, J,"

Jonny sighed, and it came out much louder than expected. Becoming flushed across his clean-shaven face, he wished that there was something he could do to show Trent his appreciation or at least save himself from the embarrassing moment.

Trent chuckled, white smile beaming as he made his way into the kitchen. Tossing the bag onto the tiles adjacent to the dishwasher, he leaned up against the same counter where the two had prepared their pre-workout shakes earlier. Spotting a stray sprinkling of powder, Trent passed a single finger through it, using his broad tongue to lick it off.

Jonny nearly fainted at the sight and memory of their close encounter.

"Damn me and my rules, eh?" Trent said achingly as he finished, the bulges in both their shorts protesting as well.

Jonny could only manage a curt nod, his eyes following Trent as he squatted to remove their dirty shaker cups from the bag. His ass was so perfect, each sweeping cheek threatening to burst out of his shorts as he loaded the dishwasher.

Damn, Jonny thought, admiring pure masculinity in motion.

Trent knew that he was being watched. After all, this wasn't his first rodeo toying with tricks. However, the chemistry he could feel percolating for Jonny certainly muddied the water (although it was safe to assume Trent would *never* use that word to describe what was going on between them).

"So," Jonny began, having regained some measure of composure, "are we doing the same thing again tonight? At Swole? We did chest, so what are we going to be working out?"

"Whoa there, eager beaver," Trent replied as he stood all the way back up. "You're so full of questions for a fuck buddy!"

Jonny slid back into his apologetic self, eyes falling to the floor even as they passed Trent's tented shorts. As Trent's hands planted themselves firmly on his own hips with his head shaking, Jonny's shoulders slumped, causing his oversized tank top to droop even more.

"Jesus, you need to work on knowing when I. Am. Joking," Trent said.

"That would be a lot easier if your face matched your mood," Jonny replied.

Trent made a sound halfway between a laugh and a scoff.

"Can't be predictable now, can I? That would mean ol' Trent Cassidy would develop a rep for being rusty."

With Jonny still hunched, Trent slipped over to him. The twenty-one-year old's head floated just above Trent's furry chest, and he stood so close that his breath billowed through Jonny's hair. Dropping his head, Trent inhaled deeply, then let out a sputtering exhale.

"Look, about… us. I have no idea what's going on. Like I told you on the way back here, most other dudes would have been gone long before ever setting foot in my house – the rules you know so well now. Each time it's quite literally get a pump, do some ruthless grinding, then adios amigo until next time. But… Hell… I don't know if it's because you're here visiting and have a way into my haven but," Trent sighed one more time, "you've gotten into my head Jonny-boy and I'm not a hundred percent sure I like it."

Jonny was a mixed bag of assorted emotions.

"Good Lord man, you look like you're about to puke. It doesn't mean I don't like you," Trent clarified, grabbing each of Jonny's shoulders. He could feel the little guy trembling like a leaf in a stiff breeze. "If that were the case, I would have beaten the shit out of you earlier when I thought you were trespassing, instead of taking you to Swole to train."

Jonny didn't laugh at the joke.

Trent grumbled.

"I'm still planning to see you the rest of this week for our sessions, that is if you still want them. And I think we've well established that you're *not* one of my regular fuck buddies."

"Well *that's* reassuring," Jonny said unenthusiastically.

Trent scowled.

"Ugh, it's just that I don't want to assume there's anything …"

"More? To us?" Jonny cut in, lifting his head so their gazes met. He could see an internal battle raging within Trent's eyes.

"Honestly, yeah."

"Look, I told you I'm not looking for anything like that either," Jonny said briskly. "Anyway, I've known you for less than a day and when I last checked this story isn't a fairy tale…"

"Far from it," Trent said as he nodded, but the action was clearly hollow. Internally, he just chalked these recent happenings up to lust – the always reliable and easy excuse – and tucked any further notions about Jonny and him having anything more, into the back of his mind.

Still ahold of Jonny, Trent glanced outside the window. It was notably lighter.

"J, what's the time?"

Jonny pulled out his phone and pressed the home button. The screen lit up, indicating that it was nearly six-thirty.

"Damn," Trent said, "time flies. The sun will be coming up soon, and both of us need to get a little rest before tackling our Sundays."

"You're right," Jonny said, still with disappointment. Despite their exchange, he liked his close-up view of Trent's fuzzy face. "Guess that means I should head upstairs. Jared wants to do some surfing today."

Trent leaned forward, hovering beside Jonny's ear.

"Not that he's very good at it," he whispered.

"Neither am I," Jonny replied with a light laugh, pausing as the fine hairs of Trent's beard stroked his cheek.

Trent pulled himself back, the look in his eyes was the same as the feeling in Jonny's chest.

Jonny stood on his tiptoes and lifted his chin, his lips approaching Trent's. But instead of meeting, they pressed against a thick finger that appeared in between.

"Remember J, there are rules here," Trent replied, pushing Jonny away with his finger before moving them to grab Jonny on that smooth chin of his. "Don't mope too much, boyo. We'll have another chance for that and more tonight. Now go on, get a couple hours of sleep before Jared wakes up and has you both turned into shark bait."

THE NEXT THREE HOURS PASSED far too quickly for Jonny, who spent most of it tossing and turning on a squeaky, flattened futon. Sleep was evasive, and the noise didn't help, but his brain was set on going a thousand miles an hour. It leaped from thoughts about his feelings for Trent – which were very confusing in their own right – over to the wildly erotic chest session they'd just had, then finally on how he was going to handle Jared for the remainder of the week.

This was supposed to be nice and simple; a relaxing getaway, Jonny thought, though he suspected Jared didn't invite him up just for a week of guiltless bro-time at bonfires and frat parties.

No, Jared had been hinting quite strongly at his own swelling feelings, especially in the flood of text messages he'd been sending over the last two weeks, punctuated with strings of kissing and heart emojis.

After Jonny had broken up with his mentally abusive ex, he didn't want to leap into another relationship. Who would want to chance that sort of heavy emotional drain coming back into their life? However, what Jonny *did* like was the attention, and so for both the right and wrong reasons, he kept the fires of flirting stoked but Jared at arm's length, using the distance between them to his advantage.

Now that he was in Logan, that defense was gone, and before the two of them had really gotten a chance to talk, Trent had swooped in, knocked Jonny off his feet with his muscles, and plowed his great big dick into Jonny's tight ass.

"What an absolute cluster," Jonny moaned, flinging a pillow over his face.

While smothered, he heard some scuffling down the hall, then weighty footsteps as they trundled up to his sparsely furnished guest room. The door was ajar.

"Hey, you up?" said an incredibly deep but groggy voice through the gap.

"Yeah, I'm up," Jonny answered; it was Jared. Throwing the pillow to the side and sitting up slightly, he yawned loudly. "Sorry, I didn't get much sleep."

"I bet," was the short reply.

Jonny could sense something was amiss.

"I'm gonna snag some water," Jared said after a moment of silence, "and head over to Café Lola's. You game? It's bottomless brunch."

"Sure, sure," Jonny replied, tossing away the covers. He clambered to his feet, and as he stretched, it dawned on him that he was still dressed in Trent's borrowed gym clothes.

Oh gosh, did Jared notice? Would he recognize the clothes? The voice in his Jonny's head was timid at first, soon booming. *Of course, you idiot, they're gym clothes for crying out loud! Not to mention you are the farthest thing in existence from a gym rat!*

Swinging his gaze toward the door, Jonny saw Jared start to lumber off; he hadn't said anything more. Jonny relaxed until he heard a very definite 'huh.'

Jonny was single and shouldn't feel like he'd stepped into a large pile of shit, yet there he was, apparently up to his knees in it. Hurriedly switching out the oversized tank top for a more fitting tee, Jonny anxiously followed, making his way for the door, down the steps, and into the kitchen. As he rounded the corner, Jonny saw Jared standing by the fridge, back toward him with a large cup in hand. He took a second to study him; the situation reversed from how he met Trent earlier that morning.

Jared was shorter than Trent (and slightly taller than Jonny was) but much beefier, his back and shoulders resembling a muscle-bound cobra.

"You done gawking?" Jared said without turning.

"Oh! Good morning," Jonny said over the sound of ice cubes falling into the plastic cup.

Jared let out a grunt as he scratched his hair, long enough to be drawn up into a mini man-bun if he wanted, but thankfully those dark brown locks were kept free and untamed.

"Not so much of a good one, then?" Jonny continued, taking a seat on one of the three barstools that lined the backside of the counter.

Drink poured, Jared turned around slowly, his suave face and blue eyes staring right at Jonny. They bore into him. Jonny wanted to look away.

"You tell me," Jared said as he inspected Jonny's clothes, noticing he'd changed. Taking a big gulp, a stream of water flowed down his scruffy neck. It continued between the slabs of his square chest, then down a deep chasm along the center of his abs, until arriving at a pair of snug red sweatpants that clung to every inch of his three powerful legs.

"W-what do you mean?" Jonny replied, wondering if this was the bullshit Trent had mentioned. It didn't take long to confirm that this was exactly the case.

"Nice outfit change," Jared answered, followed by another hydrating gulp.

"Oh," Jonny said as if caught with his hands in places they shouldn't have been (though Jared knew Trent, and it was *his* hands that often found their way inside inappropriate places).

"Yeah… oh."

Jared casually strolled up to the other side of the counter and set his cup down. Drops of condensation splattered across the marble while others trickled down the sides of the black plastic like nervous sweat.

"I just have one question for you."

Jonny felt uncomfortable; it was the cold of Jared's stare.

"Trent?"

Jonny sighed, Jared taking that to mean yes and suddenly he flew off the handle.

"Good fucking GOD, can that asshole ever just leave my shit alone…" Jared snarled. His chest was heaving, one of his hands drawn up into a tense fist.

Jonny watched the reaction unfold, trying to find the right moment so he could say something, wondering the whole time if he should.

"Are you okay?" he asked, plucking up the courage.

"Do I look it?" Jared's words lashed. "I swear that douche is always sticking his dick where it doesn't belong."

Jonny blushed guiltily.

"W-what's wrong with a little workout?" he threw out, hoping the innocence of his tone would stick.

"Really?" Jared replied skeptically. "*Really?* You're going to stand there telling me that Mr. Casanova Cassidy himself just worked out with you, after hours in that gym of his no less, with absolutely none of the fringe benefits he's got a reputation for?"

"Well, no, but…"

"Exactly!" Jared snapped again, counting along his fingers as he said, "Butts. Asses. Big dicks. Fists. Hell, even pussy. You name it, and the fucker's probably done it."

Jonny could not only sense the longstanding angst between them both, but he could see it also, straining in every tense fiber of Jared's body.

"You know brother, maybe it wasn't such a good idea for me to come up this week," Jonny murmured, rising from the stool. "I'm going to go pack and hop on one of the buses tomorrow morning and…"

"What? No!" Jared exclaimed; it was as if a calming switch flipped.

"Well, there's obviously some issues between you and Trent that I've landed right smack in the middle of and…"

Jared wet his lips and exhaled, reaching for his water.

"Yeah, there are. Look, I'm sorry man. What… and who you do on your own time is none of my business. I couldn't care less." Jared said casually.

Jonny suspected he *did* care, otherwise he wouldn't have sent the text he did just yesterday, which said: *I'm so glad it's finally time and can't wait to see you! Have a safe trip.*

Jonny recalled all the damn hearts that seemed to replace the punctuation. A part of him felt guilty that he'd jumped at the chance to spend time with Trent before Jared. Another part of him wadded the guilt up and chucked it in the trash, thinking that it was a great time.

Jared saw the thoughtful look in Jonny's eyes.

"I just wanted to spend some time getting to know you more, preferably without interference."

"Well we have today, man," Jonny said reassuringly.

"I know we do; you're not getting out of surfing that easily. It'll be a very good time, but admittedly I'm concerned about tonight."

"Why's that?"

Jared pointed toward the hall leading to the master bedroom.

"Ah, that," Jonny replied.

"Yeah. Are you planning to workout with him again?"

Jonny felt embarrassed talking so casually about sex with Jared, but answered, "Yes. We're supposed to be training again tonight."

Jared let out a slight chuckle as he downed the rest of his water. Placing the cup in the sink, he propped himself up against the counter and folded his arms.

"That almost makes it sound innocent," he said, "but, most ordinary people work out during regular hours. He's just going to fuck you again."

Wow, blunt much? Maybe I want him to, Jonny thought, knowing better than to say it.

"I just don't want to see you hurt," Jared added with genuine care. "Just be cautious with who you're dealing with, *especially* when it comes to your feelings. Trent has a knack for playing with them, especially if it gets him what he wants."

Jonny took those words to heart, even though Trent's rang out as he did.

You've gotten into my head Jonny-boy...

Surely, he wouldn't be feeding him a line just for a hole to stick his cock in? It felt more real than that.

"Besides," Jared continued, "you're a good guy, and I'm not going to let Trent stop me from having a great time this week with a great friend."

"Me either," Jonny replied, smiling.

"Well, enough depressing talk! Let's get on with the day. Bottomless brunch awaits!"

"What exactly is that?" Jonny asked as Jared worked his way around the counter toward the stairs. His eyes dawdled on Jared's ass, the red sweats like a second skin.

"It means for twenty-five bucks you can eat anything off the menu, in any order, in any amount. Why do you think I'm this big?" he replied, flexing a bicep.

"Sounds amazing."

"Trust me, it is! Okay, I'll go ahead and shower, unless you want to conserve some water now?"

"Maybe later this week?" Jonny laughed.

Jared smirked, and with a wink, he was up the stairs with more speed than a man his size should be able to muster.

As the thundering footsteps subsided, Jonny looked one last time down the hall toward Trent's room. This whole situation was so strange, and he didn't like playing both sides of the fence, but having never faced this sort of thing before – two outrageously gorgeous guys primping and preening over him like a prize – he was just cruising along to see what happened.

Then his mind started to throw curve balls…

Should I just go ahead and march down that hall to end it with Trent?

You've seen that guy, right? You want him mad or sending a fist your way?

Should I tell Jared to take a hike at brunch?

And ruin such a great friendship? Hell no.

Fine! Should I just be a man-whore for the week, get fucked by both, and see who does the better job?

Bingo! I see nothing wrong with that.

"I see everything wrong with it," Jonny muttered, running his hands through his hair as he stood there alone in his woes. "Talk about first world problems!"

Jonny knew that he wasn't that great of a catch, looking in the mirror daily reminded him of that sobering fact; the guys those two could land with a snap of their muscled fingers made up twenty of him.

So, it was then that he reluctantly (and totally against his better judgment) decided on the latter. It was the easiest route to take, all things considered. However, that assumed Jared and Trent wouldn't kill each other in the process, and something told Jonny as he looked at himself in a hall mirror that it was a very good possibility.

CHAPTER 2

BOTTOMLESS BRUNCH

THE SUN GLINTED OFF A PASSING car, causing Jared to shield his eyes.

"Hey, Tiffany?" he said to the blonde waitress, whose perkiness would be enough to make the grumpiest customer cheery, if her matching breasts failed to do the job. "Could you be a doll and close those blinds for me?"

"Sure thing," she replied in an effervescent tone, fluttering over to the windows. After a quick turn of the wand, the sun disappeared and the vibrant interior of Café Lola came back into view.

Spring break might have had the place crammed full of youngsters, Jared sitting at a small two-person table, but it was a charming place nonetheless. Bright colors and paintings adorned the walls while the scents of exotic ingredients mixed pleasantly with similar music in the air.

"Ah, that's much better," Jared said, taking a sip of pulpy orange juice as she returned. "Jonny, you decide what you're getting first?"

"There's so much on here," Jonny replied, his overloaded eyes scanning four columns of offerings. "These are small plates, right?"

Tiffany bobbed her head, and her entire body followed.

"Yep! Appetizer sized. Once you're finished, you can order more, and we'll keep bringing them out until you burst!"

"I hope it doesn't come to that," he replied, stopping at the fish tacos. "I think I'll try these, along with the… hmmm… how is the French toast?"

"It's excellent," Tiffany replied, "one of my favorite things on the menu."

"I'll take one of those then," Jonny said.

"I'll take one also," Jared added, "and a double order of sesame steak skewers."

"You got it, boys," she said, bouncing away. She glanced over her shoulder while twizzling her pen's cap playfully between her teeth.

"Well, well, someone likes us," Jared whispered, involuntarily flexing his back. "But she would say the French toast was her favorite thing, wouldn't she? I bet they have to say that regardless of what's asked about."

"You mean she likes *you*," Jonny replied sensitively. "Who wouldn't though, that v-neck is so small you've not only got people covered who like to ogle studs, but who like to admire toddlers as well."

Jared looked at Jonny, directly across from him, and observed his nerdy outfit: an off-white *Pokémon* tee and skinny jeans. He thought it suited Jonny much better than a jumbo tank top and musty gym shorts. Since it was truly 'him' and that's what made it great.

"It doesn't matter too much does it, considering she's not our type?" Jared answered grumpily. "Besides, I happen to find shirts this size *very* comfortable."

"You would. So, does ..."

Jonny suddenly stopped; he was about to mention Trent.

Jared wasn't stupid, though in the interest of keeping things cool he tried to hide his annoyance. That was difficult at best.

"Speaking of *jerks*," he said, squashing an obstinate silence that started to form while threatening to launch an argument, "is the ex-boyfriend totally out of the picture now?"

"Fred?" Jonny answered, relieved Jared wasn't pressing him on Trent, but his face cringed, and lips curled anyway from the mere mention of his ex's name. "Yeah, that bastard's history as of the middle of last week."

Jared looked relieved, though it could be read as pleased.

"Good, you deserve much better than that loser."

"Do I?"

"What?" Jared asked. He was expecting agreement and didn't know quite what to say.

"Sometimes I wonder if I do deserve better…" Jonny continued, melancholy. "It feels like my lot in life. As I work my butt off in all sorts of this things – trying to be successful at them – love, classes, you name it, the only success I seem to be reaping is getting shafted in the end. Not the good kind either. Geez, I swear it feels like I have 'fuck me over' tattooed on my forehead. The very least these people could do is have the courtesy to lube up beforehand."

Jared pretended to inspect the area in detail, complete with an invisible magnifying glass.

"Nope, no letters as far as I can see," he replied, and Jonny smiled. "Look, all this hard work will all pay off in the end. Life has hurdles, and everyone is different. You're just facing more now rather than later, I'm sure of it."

A supportive hand made its way from Jared's side of the table, navigating napkins, flatware, and condiments before settling on top of Jonny's.

Jonny's eyes flicked downward.

"Jared, I…"

"You don't think I know that you've been keeping me at bay?"

"It's all the hearts," Jonny said half-laughing.

"Yeah, I love those, probably too much eh?" Jared smirked. "But seriously, I can't blame you for needing your space. I told you back at the house that you're a good guy, one of the best I know, and Fred definitely did a number on you up here."

Jared tapped his temple with his free hand, and Jonny looked off to a distant part of the café.

"You're hurt from those experiences," Jared continued. "Anybody would be, but I'm not going to lie: I like you, a lot. I just want you to know from the bottom of my heart to the top of your aching one: I'm here for you, should you need me."

Jonny pulled his hand away, complicated feelings and thoughts raging once more.

Why is this shit never easy?

Instead of withdrawing further, Jonny placed his hand back on top of Jared's and rubbed it with his thumb.

"Thank you," he replied, "it's great knowing that I have you as a friend."

"I could be more than a friend if you wanted…" he hinted, smiling.

"I… I will think about it," Jonny answered, his mind already contemplating how much harder the week was going to be on him than he thought.

"That's all I ask," Jared replied as Tiffany returned with their first round of food.

CHAPTER 3

THE CARB UP

"I FEEL LIKE A PIECE of meat," Jonny said as he bobbed around in his seat, unrelenting potholes seeming to have multiplied during the day.

He'd been talking with Trent about his day, which had been going great with Jared until half an hour ago.

Expecting a snarky reply from Trent, Jonny was surprised when he didn't get one.

"You pretty much are," Trent replied bluntly.

"Thanks," Jonny said disapprovingly.

"You're welcome. I wouldn't dwell on it or worry too much, though; Jared will get over it. He always does."

Jonny slowly turned his head toward Trent, placing a hand on his jeans-covered thigh and giving it a light squeeze.

Earlier, Jared had a confrontation with Trent and suffice to say: it wasn't pretty. He was trying to get Jonny to go with him to a party over at a local frat house, but Jonny had already committed to another workout session with Trent (for the entire week, in fact). So, instead of things going smoothly, that's when the posturing between the two muscle-heads escalated.

Trent insisted Jonny wasn't missing out and Jared was using the day's fun in an attempt to guilt Jonny into going to the party while telling Trent to keep his dick zipped up in his pants.

To Jonny, the arguing made him feel like he was smack in the middle of his old relationship again and he just wanted to tell them both to fuck off, pack his bags, and call a cab to the bus station.

But, he didn't, Trent's fucking lustful stare anchoring his feet to the floor of the house while Jared's friendly face did the same.

Jonny was torn (and shouldn't have been), ultimately deciding on his original commitment to Trent. Jared wasn't happy about it at all, storming off to the party by himself without another word. The look of disappointment on his face, along with the echoing sting of the slamming door managed to stick with Jonny.

"I'm sorry about all that back at the house," Trent continued, drawing Jonny's attention back to the present. "What you've been seeing between us is nothing new. It fucking sucks balls, and I guess the fact you're a mutual buddy is amplifying his tirades."

Jonny could only focus on one word in that entire sentence.

"Buddy?" he spat.

"Dude, I wasn't talking about *that* kind of buddy," Trent was quick to say defensively. "On second thought, aren't you both kinds now? Making you a bi-buddy, or bi-bud? Which do you prefer Jonny-boy?"

"Ugh! There's the real Trent; knew he wouldn't be gone for long. Away with your truths," Jonny barked, yanking his hand away from Trent's leg only to have it snatched back into position. He turned his head and looked out of the window with a small smile.

A few blissful minutes went by.

"Hey, Trent…"

"Yeah, *buddy?*"

"You're hilarious... not. I was just wondering if we were still heading over to Swole now; I don't remember seeing any of this stuff we're passing, but I guess you might have had me a little distracted the first time."

"Seems like I'm doing that now," Trent observed, spotting a tent in Jonny's shorts. "Tell little John it'll be playtime soon enough, but damn you're observant. The Summerset Center is still a bit further north; I'm taking you west for something big to eat."

"Eat?" Jonny asked with surprise, his head spinning back around while flashes of steak skewers came back to haunt him. "So, we aren't working out then?"

"Oh, you bet that beautiful ass of yours we are," Trent replied. "I'm not letting you off that easily. In fact, I think I was far too gentle with you for chest, so we're hitting the other end of the spectrum: body part most hate so much they skip working out entirely."

"I'm almost afraid to ask what that is," Jonny said, still sore across both his chest and lower body.

"Legs," Trent replied with an evil smile.

Jonny looked down to his hand which was still caressing that massive hunk of meat Trent had as a limb.

"Oh shit," he mumbled, Trent chuckling.

"Gosh, you're so worrisome. I'm not going to force you to move the same amount of weight I do, but it's still not going to be easy."

"Not sure I want to do it now."

"You want the rewards, don't you?"

Jonny nodded eagerly, followed by a hard swallow.

"Well then, in order to do it right, we have to get fueled up properly," Trent said. "Which is why I'm taking you for something to eat."

Jonny still thought the whole idea was odd.

"Not every meathead thinks the same way," Trent continued, donning his personal trainer's hat. "Some nut jobs train fasted, but I'm a big believer in carbing up before leg and back days since they're heavier lifts." He smirked. "The kind you should like: *brutal*."

Parts of Jonny tensed up, while others quivered with the thought.

"Here I thought I did well enough to get through that chest workout, and you're telling me that it's going to get worse."

"Haha, you did do well," Trent replied. "Don't go doubting that one bit, but yeah, it's going to be worse for you tonight and in a way, much better."

"If you say so. It sounds horrifying."

Jonny didn't know if it was butterflies in his stomach or just the thought of eating something substantial that late (spurred by his gluttonous session with Jared) but he was put off by the idea.

"Sounds to me like you're just asking to be sick," Jonny said, hoping the thought of vomit would steer Trent toward Swole. But this was Trent Cassidy he was talking to, and Jonny should have known better by now.

"Puking on leg day?" Trent replied. "That's the ultimate badge of honor."

"Of course it is," Jonny said, thinking that gym rats were some of the hottest, yet strangest people around.

Trent flicked the turn signal and spun the wheel, his '69 Charger gliding across the lanes into a parking lot, which was surprisingly busy for ten o'clock.

Jonny leaned forward as the car came to a stop between two pickup trucks, looking at the packed building ahead, the lights of a garish sign dancing across the glass.

"The Lard Have Mercy?" he said sardonically. "I swear Trent, folks in this town have the weirdest names for places."

"There's nothing weird about LHM," Trent retorted, serious as if his mother was slandered. "Besides, it's a well-known chain that started in Houston, so don't go blaming Logan for that."

"*I've* never heard of it."

"That's because you've been sheltered in that tiny town you live in, but you're about to get acquainted with some of the best burgers around."

"We could have just gone to Mc –"

Trent's hand shot up, a single finger raised.

"No. Fucking. Way. That place isn't in the same category; you'll see." Trent's voice shifted from admonishment to admiration. "This place has the best food and some of the largest burgers in the country. Heard stories of some guy named Gage in Texas, ate the Colossal King in less than ten minutes. That's like nearly two pounds of beef. Shit, I've never made it past the Royal Triple Decker. Bet his pump was immense."

"And I bet the toilet screamed immensely too," Jonny chuckled. He liked seeing Trent's enthusiasm; it suited him. Hopefully, it was something he would see more. "Okay, you've convinced me. Just be sure you wait until later before you go and have an orgasm unless this Gage does it for you."

Trent grabbed the door handle and popped it open, letting some of the warm night air slip into the cab.

"Please. I thought you knew me by now. Just for that, you're going to make sure I cum twice tonight."

Jonny liked the sound of that threat, opening his door and easing his way outside. Trent wasn't far behind and together, they both made their way to the entrance.

JONNY SAT WITH HIS EYES wide open, the collection of plates laid out in front of them glistening with grease and smelling divine. It was, in a word: heaven.

The joint was extremely busy and full of cheers and good times, spring break contributing a lot to that, plus the extended hours for the week.

Trent was a beast, shoveling fries and bites of eggy patties into his mouth like a front loader while managing to keep his beard pristine. Jonny, on the other hand, pecked at his quarter-pounder like a pigeon.

"We aren't leaving until you finish that," Trent said with his mouth stuffed, swallowing a straw full of water to wash it down. "You are gonna need the energy."

Jonny took a big bite, grease dribbling down his chin into the napkin unfolded across his lap. Trent's eyes followed it, and Jonny smirked, taking another mouthful. More grease stained the napkin below the table.

"Liking what you see?" Jonny asked.

"More like what I can't see right now," Trent replied, his mischievous eyes darting over to a lone saucer on his right. On it was a single, unadorned hotdog bun.

Jonny eyed it, too.

"That was a strange thing to order," he said, considering the rest of the plates were loaded down. "I thought you'd have gotten a hot dog with it."

Trent smiled as if waiting for that as a signal. He looked around and took his hands off the burger, lowering them both beneath the table.

Watching him fidget as if handling a whopper, Jonny rose in his seat to get a better view.

Trent's look was pure sin, his hands full of hard cock, the tip glistening.

Jonny fell back onto his side of the stiff booth.

"Are you serious right now?" Jonny whispered harshly. "Have you seen how many people are in here? Someone is going to see you!"

Trent shrugged, moving one of his hands down the thick shaft and back up again. Using his thumb, he rubbed the slick precum over his head and let out a little moan, generating more. Reaching for the hot dog bun, a long gossamer strand stretched in between.

Holy shit, Jonny thought. *This is so wrong!*

And he liked every fucking second of it.

Grabbing the bun, Trent brought it down to his lap where he unfolded it, wrapping his stiff dick with the soft bread.

"I'm ready," he said to Jonny.

"W-what? Ready for what?"

"I told you, *you're* getting me off twice tonight."

Jonny's heart began beating faster, his eyes scanning the room. He was sure the couple across from them knew what was going on. Maybe the woman over at the counter. Or the man just off and behind him to the left. He couldn't breathe, especially when his gaze returned to Trent.

"Now," Trent said. "Take off your shoes."

Jonny hesitated, but as Trent leaned forward, growling, he complied. Slipping out of his sneakers, Jonny wiggled his sock-clad toes.

"Now, bring them up here," Trent ordered.

Jonny eased himself down in the booth, lifting his legs into Trent's lap. He felt his rough hands grab hold of his ankles, pushing his feet closer together until they met the bun. Trent then started to move them up and down, the bun sliding along his unyielding shaft.

"That's it, Jonny-boy," Trent said with a slight rasp. "Work it."

Jonny was sure someone was watching, he could feel eyes on him. There was no tablecloth, their wicked activity exposed for anyone who happened to look in their direction.

"Fuck whoever sees," Trent said, noting Jonny's distractions. "You're attention. On me. Now."

Jonny gulped, focusing on his movement along Trent's dick. It felt incredibly awkward yet hot as fuck. He added a slight twist to each up and down stroke, Trent obviously satisfied.

The precum started to gush, flowing down into the now soggy bun. Jonny didn't care, he kept churning, cranking moan after pleasurable moan from his trainer. Then it dawned on him: he was in control at that moment.

Hearing distant murmurs, Jonny closed his eyes and carried on, forgetting that he was in a crowded restaurant while changing rhythm unpredictably, ecstasy surging into Trent's aching loins.

"Oh fuck," Trent uttered, long and agonizingly slow. "You're fucking good at... oh, fuck!"

Jonny could tell Trent was close, his feet now up against raw cock as he continued to stroke Trent off.

"Yeah, you like that big guy?" Jonny muttered.

"Fuck yeah I do. Oh God, I'm about to... oh yeah, you've done it. I'm about to cum."

Jonny opened his eyes, the feeling of Trent's dick causing his own cock to drool the entire time, the scene in his shorts a slick mess. He could feel Trent stiffening, throbbing, convulsing as ropes of streaming white splattered against his dark tank top.

Trent was panting heavily, sweat beaded on his brow.

Glancing at the couple across from them, Jonny spotted the man looking in their direction. He made a subtle thumbs-up gesture before returning his attention to his girlfriend who, surprisingly, hadn't noticed a thing. Amused and somewhat in disbelief, Jonny looked back at Trent; his shirt was disastrous like a large napkin smothered in greasy stains.

"Good job, Jonny-boy," Trent said, his beard finally dirty. "Number one down; one more to go."

Sitting upright, Jonny was rather proud of himself, but he didn't get much of a chance to think about it before their waiter returned. His heart fluttered as the waiter glanced disapprovingly at Trent's shirt, and he prepared himself to be thrown out of the place.

"My goodness you must have hated the food; you're quite the messy eater, aren't you?" the waiter said with a titter. "Sauce and grease are everywhere."

Jonny laughed along with him while Trent cleared away the stray sauce from his beard.

"I'm the messiest of them all," he said smugly, looking devilishly at Jonny. "I think we are ready for the check please."

CHAPTER 4

ASS TO GRASS

"**I STILL CANNOT BELIEVE YOU,**" Jonny said, head shaking as the two pulled into the Summerset Center.

"Just being me," Trent said assertively. "What I can't believe is you didn't even finish that little bitty burger. The thing should be on the kid's menu."

"And you're just going to work out as if you didn't just eat the entire adult menu?"

Trent switched off the engine and looked right at Jonny.

"You bet," he said, lifting a new tank top he had changed into. His abs, on the other hand, looked unchanged.

"Jesus, you don't even have a food baby," Jonny said, reaching out to feel Trent's stomach; it was as hard as ever, each ridge demanding to be touched at least once. Maybe twice (especially the lower ones). "Dammit, I really hate your genetics."

"My other tank top does too," he smirked. "Come on, squats are calling."

Squats, Jonny thought. The name itself was dirty, but he was excited to find out what Trent's spin on the night would be. If it was anything like last time, traditional was not the word to apply to any of this.

The two got out of the car, Trent working his way in ahead of Jonny. He didn't mind being left to follow again, appreciating the persistent view of Trent's ass as it swished hypnotically in those shorts.

"You know, I just realized the highly appropriate color of your sign," Jonny observed, the red lights of the gym's thick lettering calling out like a beacon of sin in the night.

"Mhmm," Trent answered as he opened the door and switched off the alarm. "Care to get the lights again?"

"Sure," Jonny said, heading over to the right to flip the switch.

Once again, the lights flickered to life, and Trent's private playground appeared out of the darkness.

"Remember him?" Trent asked as they walked through toward the locker rooms, pointing in the direction of the leg area on the left. A squat rack sat in the center. "We're gonna get some work done on that later."

Jonny eyed the machine, recalling it from last time. Tonight, its black metal frame looked far more intimidating.

"Yup, remember *brutal* is the word. Nothing like the tanning booth…"

Jonny trembled with good memories, looking over at the booth's locked door.

"And no worries for you this time on us being interrupted by Lisa." Trent stopped just ahead of the locker room door, putting a hand on Jonny's shoulder before sliding it down the length of his upper arm. "You're *all mine*."

With that, he grabbed hold and guided Jonny into the room, its gray walls and blue lockers welcoming them back. Tossing his bag on one of the wooden benches in the middle he turned, pushing Jonny up against a bank of cold metal with one hand, slamming the other next to his head. Before Jonny could even say a word, Trent had moved in to kiss him, the two locking lips for a couple of minutes.

"You should change your shorts; still messy from the restaurant," Trent said, pulling away just as quickly as he'd rushed in, leaving Jonny wobbly against the locker. He rifled through his gym bag, tossing over a clean pair.

"Do you always keep spare clothes in your gym bag?"

Trent looked at Jonny saying, "I swear, once I think that you've finally worked out the kind of guy I am, you prove me wrong. What I don't have in here, I have in some of those locker's you're trembling against."

"Sorry, it's just cold."

"Yeah, sure it is," Trent said as he watched Jonny change, his dick flopping around as he pulled the new pair up. "Didn't look all that cold to me."

"Whatever. So, are you going to change?"

Without another word, Trent lowered his onion skin shorts, his massive meat dangling heavily. Walking over to the locker next to Jonny, he reached in and pulled out a pair of sweat shorts that looked amazing on him.

"You really do have all this down to a science, don't you?"

"Fuck yes I do," Trent replied and with a wink added, "I even pay Lisa extra to do my gym laundry."

Jonny couldn't manage anything but a light smile, shaking his head in disbelief.

"I told you she knows me well," Trent said. "Now, help me get these on."

Jonny blinked, half expecting to get another show from behind, full of tight hamstrings and sculpted ass.

"Wait, what?"

"You heard me," he answered, dropping the shorts to the floor and placing one foot in them. "I need some help getting them on."

Jonny sunk to his knees, the tile floor uncomfortable. Nonetheless, he guided Trent's foot into one of the leg holes, followed by the other. As he lifted them up and over his calves, he could feel something tapping against the top of his head. Raising his gaze, he saw that it was Trent, slapping his semi-hard cock against him.

Continuing, Jonny stretched the shorts over Trent's mammoth thighs, and once the elastic was just beneath his crotch, Jonny stopped. Leaning forward, he buried his nose in Trent's bull-sized balls, spreading those two generous orbs to each side as he inhaled, bathing them with his tongue at the same time. The powerful, masculine scent spurred him on, and he lifted the shorts some more. They soon covered his balls, riding higher up the shaft. Jonny used his tongue to pave a smooth path all the way up those nine inches to tip, where a shiny reward waited. Jonny lapped it up amidst several moans, sucking on the head to draw out every remaining drop before sealing the package away.

"That's a good boy," Trent said boldly, pushing Jonny's face into his shorts. "Now it's time to get started."

JONNY WAS ALREADY ABOUT TO lose it by the time they'd even made it to the gym floor, Trent heading down a little way before turning right into the leg room.

Shit, I hope I make it through tonight, he said to himself as he stepped onto the spongy mats, worried that if Trent so much as looked at him the wrong way he would cum instantly.

That feeling went away as Jonny surveyed the room. There were metal dumbbells along the wall to the right, but what drew his eyes was all the daunting equipment. Plate-loaded machines (the squat rack, a Smith machine, and a leg press to name a few) stood front and center while other machines (for leg extension, curls, and the like) were to his left. Between the metal jungle was a series of weight trees, each ladened with iron plates ranging from five up to forty-five pounds.

"Well, it's official," Jonny said. "I've already shit myself."

Trent laughed as he made way over to the leg extensions.

"We'll start here," he said, repositioning the backrest and taking a seat. The taunt vinyl squeaked as Trent adjusted himself and grabbing the pin, he placed it all the way down the stack. Positioning the padded lower bar just above his ankles, he said, "I normally do sets of single then double-legged extensions, but tonight we'll only go through four sets of doubles, okay?"

"Don't tell me you're already going easy?"

"No, but you should consider it a thank you for helping me so well with my shorts."

Trent then set about cranking out his set, scowling by the time he was on the last few reps. With a pained groan and a loud *clang*, he finished, legs throbbing as he struggled to stand.

"Your turn," he said, pointing at the seat.

Jonny took his time, feeling like he was climbing into an electric chair. The feeling didn't subside as he raised the pin to about eighty pounds (Trent was doing two-hundred-fifty).

The first few raises weren't all that bad until Trent instructed him to, "Squeeze those quads at the top."

That's when the searing burn started, increasing with each repetition. It was painful, but also somewhat pleasing, particularly when Trent placed a hand on one of Jonny's thighs to make sure he was doing as he was told.

Jonny floundered.

"I didn't say stop," Trent snarled. "Give me two more… that's it… one… and… good."

When the weights came crashing down, releasing Jonny from their grasp, his legs were tingling, and he had great difficulty standing.

"What were you saying about me going easy, bro? That was just set number one," Trent said as he watched Jonny woozily brace himself on a nearby piece of equipment. "We still have three more to go."

With rugged grunts, some yells, and a few cuss words, the two of them made their way through the rest of the leg extensions. By the end, Trent's legs had lost some of their definition but were unbelievably swollen and veiny as a result. Jonny tried his best to trace all the crossing lines with his eyes, but there were so many of them that he lost track.

Fuck my life, he thought. *That's hot!*

"You like my personal road maps?" Trent joked as he made his way over to a mat that was typically used for deadlifts. "Use 'em to find your way over here."

"Yeah, they're great," Jonny replied as he wet his lips, watching Trent grab one of the pre-weighted barbells off a pyramidal rack. Even though they weren't working out arms, his seem to be engorged. "I don't know how you don't spend all day looking at yourself in the mirror."

"You flatter me, boyo," Trent said, throwing the bar across his upper back. "Lunges next. Four sets, ten to fifteen reps."

He stepped forward with one leg and plunged, lowering himself until the opposing knee touched the mat. Then, after a brief pause, he pushed himself back up.

Jonny watched, trying to focus on form, but all he could see was Trent's ass popping out like some ripe peach at the bottom and clenching tightly at the top of the movement. Trent repeated the process with the other leg and got into a smooth back and forth rhythm until all fifteen reps per leg were done.

"You made that look really easy," Jonny said, snatching a lighter bar off the same rack to use. Trying to duplicate what he saw Trent doing, Jonny struggled at times to get back off the floor.

"That was a good job for your first try. Just make sure you keep your core tight, and you should be set," Trent noted. "It'll help your form and the ability to get your ass back up."

Jonny breathed heavily while nodding, noticing Trent's shorts were soaked up front.

"Sweating so much already?" he asked playfully.

"It's not sweat," Trent said, dipping into his next set.

Jonny rubbed the back of his neck bashfully until it was his turn again.

Once those draining sets of lunges were out of the way, Trent took Jonny through a round on both the abductor and adductor machines. Typically machines that discouraged eye contact with those using them, Trent and Jonny gave each other sideways glances as their legs spread open in compromising positions.

"Those machines are far more fun with women," Trent said casually, wagging his tongue as he arrived at the lying leg curl machine.

Jonny didn't say anything, putting a thumb in his mouth as he watched Trent getting into position on his stomach. The man set the weight and immediately curled his legs upward.

"Watch my form carefully," he said between grunts and timed breaths. "You're going to have to duplicate it perfectly before we move onto the final routine."

"Seems easy enough," Jonny replied. "I'm am glad we're lying down for these."

Trent answered with a wry smirk, surveying every inch of Jonny as he got into position.

After a few reps with surprisingly good form, Jonny could feel Trent's gaze boring into him again. Out of the corner of an eye, he could see Trent working the front of his shorts, and soon, he had positioned himself mere inches in front of Jonny. That massive cock was struggling to get out of those shorts.

"Don't stop," Trent scolded. "That could be a dangerous thing."

Jonny bowed his head obediently and continued with his sets. That's when he felt Trent's massive weight settle on top of him, that hard dick resting against the back of his head while Trent's hands and face made way for Jonny's ass.

"Keep going," Trent directed, his hands caressing then kneading Jonny's cheeks as they moved his shorts down, exposing his silky, smooth skin.

Trent groaned as he spread those cheeks apart, getting a glimpse of that treasured hole he'd been craving. He brushed his beard along the dividing line, causing Jonny to falter.

"Tsk, tsk. There's that bad form creeping in," Trent grumbled, continuing his bearded assault.

"It's y-your f-fault," Jonny stammered, eyes rolling back into his head. He could barely breathe from the strain of the curls plus Trent's body on top of his.

"Don't blame my facial hair for your hiccups."

Jonny would have retorted, but he could only manage a long moan, the soft bristles surrounding Trent's mouth hovering precariously over his tender breach. He could feel his breath; he was so close.

"Oh… that feels good…" Jonny groaned, feeling a spit-lubed finger circling, then plunging into his depths. It rifled around, seeking his prostrate like a guided missile and once it made contact, Jonny exploded with shuddering grace.

His legs fell, and the weights crashed, Trent adding a second, then a third finger to explore.

"Fuck!" Jonny roared, his dick salivating while trapped between him and the machine's padding. "I'm getting close…"

Trent ignored him, his fingers doing all the answering on his behalf.

"T-Trent, s-stop." Jonny writhed. "I'm… I'm going to…"

The wild scream that followed shook the building, all four of Trent's fingers diving in just as Jonny's dick pumped out hot and sticky pools that drenched his shorts.

Jonny collapsed, the full weight of Trent's sweaty body crushing him.

"Congrats," Trent whispered. "You've earned squat time."

IT TOOK JONNY NEARLY TEN minutes to recuperate now that Trent was off him. The vinyl was almost refreshing against his body, like the cold side of a pillow that had just been flipped over. He could have stayed there for another ten minutes, but something told him that Trent wouldn't be too pleased with that amount of laziness in his gym.

Looking around while still on his belly, Jonny didn't immediately see Trent, but could hear him loading the squat rack. Grudgingly standing, Jonny looked toward the center of the room and saw the big guy putting three forty-five pound plates on one side of the bar, moving on to the other. The weight was impressive, but Trent doing it all stark naked was even more.

"Hey sleepy head," Trent called as the first plate slammed into position. His body didn't even look worn or tired. "All rested up?"

"Yeah," Jonny replied blearily, trying his best to stop himself from yawning, the second plate banging into place helping on that front. "I hope you're not expecting me to lift all that?"

"What, three-forty-five too much for you?" Trent prodded as he shifted the last plate into position, placing a padded cylinder around the middle of the bar afterward. "I figured we could knock my sets out as usual then I could focus on you."

Jonny liked Trent's idea of focusing, moving closer to the squat rack. Looking closer at the setup up, it looked downright scary, like some medieval torture device.

"I don't think I need a spot," Trent said as he positioned himself with the pad across the upper part of his back and his arms out to the sides, grasping the bar. "But be on standby just in case."

"What's that mean?" Jonny asked, completely drawing a blank.

"It means I might need you to help guide me, but I normally do this weight fairly easily for sets of ten."

To his surprise, Jonny started to stir below his shorts again, dick growing at the thought that Trent was about to move weight that was essentially equivalent to more than two of him, across his back.

"You know what would help to motivate me?" Trent asked.

Jonny shook his head rapidly.

"You taking off those clothes."

"Me?" Jonny hesitated.

"Yes you," Trent said. "I swear these sessions are making you deaf. Take them off then step a little over to my right. I want to see you in the mirror as I do these."

Slowly, Jonny took off the tank top, revealing his lean body and when he slid off those tainted shorts, Trent made a distinct grunt as Jonny's growing chub came into view.

Fucking hell, Trent thought as he wiped his lips with a couple of those thick fingers, drooling at the size difference of Jonny's David to his Goliath.

"Much better," Trent said, lifting the weight then stepping back a couple of paces.

Jonny stared in amazement as Trent dropped toward the floor, his ass nearly touching the mat before he strained and shouted back up to the top. Every fiber in his legs jittered with stress as it underwent rep after rep, the fibers being worn and torn to come back bigger and even stronger than before. As Trent pounded through his routine, Jonny's hand gripped the base of his dick and started stroking, getting to full length by the time Trent had finished his third and final set.

"I appreciate that," he said, striding up to Jonny. "A lot."

Taking him into his massive arms, he brought him close and gave him a kiss on the neck, working his way up to his lips. As their chests touched, each could feel the heartbeat of the other, racing in sheer enjoyment. Jonny leaped up and wrapped his legs around Trent's large ones, propped up to receive one of the most passionate French kisses of his life.

"Okay, you big distraction," Trent said, lowering Jonny to his bare feet. "Your turn. I'll help you take off some of the weights."

"How about all of them?" Jonny said with a laugh, having been nervous about doing squats at all.

"I know that you're not a pussy," Trent said offhandedly, removing two plates from his side.

Jonny did the same, realizing how heavy each plate was tonight.

Maybe I should have eaten that burger, he thought.

"Alright, I'm going to spot you on these," Trent said, one-hundred-thirty-five pounds left on the bar. "It might be heavy for you as a beginner, but I think with my help you'll be able to get it. We can adjust if need be after the first set. Plus, the safety guards are there on each side in case we fall."

God, I hope we do, Jonny wished to himself, getting into position beneath the bar. The pad was rougher than he thought it would be and the entire thing felt precarious, not to mention that he felt frail as fuck upon seeing his reflection, Trent's shoulders and outer thighs peeking out from either side.

"Now some things before we get going," Trent said, stepping closer and into his spotter's position. "This is dangerous, so I will stay close to you and the bar. Dump the bar off your back *only* as an absolute last resort, okay?"

It was hard for Jonny to concentrate, the smell and feel of Trent's hard muscles against his back while his dick was pointed down, nestled nicely between his cheeks.

"You get that?" Trent asked. "I need to hear you say it."

"Yes," Jonny replied meekly.

"Okay," Trent said, taking a single step back while lowering his hands by Jonny's waist. "Now lift."

Jonny pushed up, the weight now resting solely on his shoulders, the two stepped back from the assembly, where Jonny billowed like a stiff stick in the breeze.

"And down," Trent said, following Jonny as he squatted.

Jonny's legs buckled slightly as his thighs became parallel to the floor. Trent was quick to move, hands grasping Jonny's chest while his arms helped stabilize then lift him back to standing.

"Sorry," Jonny said nervously.

"No worries," Trent reassured him. "Let's try again."

Starting over, Jonny managed to plow through a good set of eight reps before his legs gave out. Walking slowly back to the rest position, they set the bar down, clanking, and Jonny relaxed.

"Holy moly," he said, "that was more intense than I thought."

"Agreed. Let's take the weights off so I can show you how to get better form and your ass to the grass so to speak."

With the plates gone, the bar only weighed forty-five pounds, which would be much more manageable for the remainder of the set. The two repositioned themselves to go through another set.

This time, Trent didn't step away, keeping himself planted firmly against Jonny. He hooked his arms beneath Jonny's armpits, grabbing hold of his pecs while his dick, still free and expectant, returned to its resting place down the center of Jonny's ass.

The two squatted together, reaching parallel then beyond, Jonny moaning as his ass neared the floor; the strain from the previous set starting to set his legs on fire. Making him feel even warmer, he could feel Trent's thick cock grinding against him, throbbing more powerfully as they repeated the process seven more times.

"Good boy," Trent muttered as they rested. "I think one more set should do it."

Jonny was aching, but also excited, his dick still rigid even after the leg curl incident.

Grabbing the bar, they both got into position. However, this time, as Jonny started his descent, Trent spat on his dick and pushed it all the way into Jonny's ass. They both bellowed, each sensation rivaling the other for superiority – Jonny's hole versus Trent's girth.

"Fuck, you're tight," Trent mumbled, breathing hard as he took the opportunity for a few lengthy strokes. "Oh shit, that feels good."

Jonny was unable to reply, ecstasy taking over through the combination of leg pain and his ass getting tore up by a nine by seven-inch rod.

"Alright Jonny-boy, it's time to squat. If my dick falls out of you, you're going to have to start that rep over again."

Jonny didn't mind if that meant more of this, but he went down slowly, making sure to stay filled the entire way down. At the bottom, Trent slid out ("Oh, fuck yeah!") then thrust himself back in a couple of times ("Take it, yeah all the way!"). Again and again, they squatted as Trent fucked, harder and harder until Jonny's legs were damn near breaking.

On the last rep, Trent kept Jonny locked in place, and he was unable to stand as Trent had his way with him, grunting and grinding until Jonny was nearly in tears from the pain and his ass reddened from being reamed.

With a great moan, Trent released him and Jonny shot up, stepping forward to rest on the bar. Trent didn't give him a second before he was on, then inside him again. His arms grasped Jonny's hips as he fucked, those huge nuts slapping against Jonny's skin.

Jonny had propped himself against the bar, watching himself heave and convulse in the mirror, sweat flowing down his entire body, joining ample amounts of precum as it all flicked off his bouncing dick against the glass.

God, it was a mess, and both men reveled in it.

"Fuck, Jonny-boy," Trent said, his stamina rising as more blood surged into his already swollen dick, screaming in near skin-splitting agony as he slid around inside Jonny's velvety asshole. "I'm not going to cum until I see you do…"

Jonny reached for his dick, Trent lashing a hand out to force him back to the bar.

"No hands!" he roared. "I'm gonna force it out of you."

"But I can't," Jonny pleaded, trying to glance over his shoulder to get a glimpse of Trent so he could beg him to stop… even though part of him didn't want to. "I've never…."

More precum splattered against the gym mirror, Jonny's cock saying that he damn well could.

"Look at your fucking self," Trent said, grabbing the back of Jonny's head and forcing him to look straight on again. "Stop doubting yourself and just… fucking… do it!"

Jonny oozed even more precum, long ropes of it helicoptering as his hard dick bounced around.

Trent was relentless, working himself up into a dripping fury. He continued rolling his hips, cock working overtime to bring every pleasurable sensation to Jonny that he could, while holding himself off from spilling over.

"Oh God…" Jonny muttered.

"Yeah, baby!"

"Oh God!"

"Come on!"

"OH GOD!"

Jonny shook, jets of jizz flying from the end of his cock, splashing against the glass before running down in thick, cloudy streaks.

"Yeah, my turn," Trent said, at last free to release.

Pulling out and setting his hard meat against Jonny's back, he spurted, sending streams of white, hot cum up into the air. He struck himself in the chin twice and soaked the back of Jonny's head.

"Holy shit!" Trent exclaimed, still going as he licked his lips, chuckling with pride. "Motherfucker, *that* was a first."

Both stood there, literally drained and panting.

"That was incredible," Jonny huffed, barely able to stand. If he weren't still holding onto the bar, he would have fallen over.

Trent hugged him, their sticky bodies entwined.

"Damn we're nasty," he said.

"So?" Jonny replied.

"Exactly."

Kissing Jonny's neck, Trent took a deep breath.

"Night's still fairly young; you want me to take you to see Jared over at R&E?"

"Nah," Jonny replied. "I'm okay right here. I'll talk with him tomorrow."

"He's attracted to you and then some, you know that right?"

Jonny nodded, reaching up to muss Trent's hair.

"I know, and I don't want to hurt him."

"This isn't going to end well if you keep stringing him along."

"For who?"

"Damn son," Trent chuckled, "taking notes from my playbook, are you?"

"Well, I see it ending one of three ways," Jonny continued. "You end up killing him for me, he ends up killing you for me, or…"

"Yeah?" Trent said, his interest piqued.

"You and he are both going to fuck the shit out of me."

Trent laughed, having never thought once about Jared in that capacity.

"Well, I don't know about *that*."

"Fine, don't believe me. You know one thing you can't deny, though?" Jonny asked, Trent once again giving him a suspicious eye. "Lisa is going to kill you when she arrives in the morning."

THE END

ABOUT THE AUTHOR

In the beginning, Golden worked the standard corporate rat race, completing college with a chemical engineering degree before starting a small photography company on the side.

Since then, the FuriousFotog brand grew into an internationally recognized brand, published in both domestic and international magazines, on websites, and trade/e-book book covers (even appearing on some himself).

Having been in the industry since 2012, Golden has interfaced and networked with countless other authors, clients, and photographers to license and create over 400 romance book cover images, diversifying into commercial work as well.

He published his debut novel, Homeward Bound (Journeyman 1) in June 2016, completing the six-book series in January 2017.

Website: www.onefuriousfotog.com

Facebook (Photography): www.facebook.com/furiousfotog

Facebook (Author): www.facebook.com/authorgoldenczermak

Newsletter: http://eepurl.com/b5p5if

OTHER BOOKS BY THE AUTHOR

NOW AVAILABLE:
Homeward Bound (Journeyman Series One)
Seal of Solomon (Journeyman Series Two)
Made to Suffer (Journeyman Series Three)
The Devil's Highway (Journeyman Series Four)
Then Hell Followed (Journeyman Series Five)
Running on Empty (Journeyman Series Six)
Swole Chest Day

NOVELS TO LOOK OUT FOR:
The Steam Tycoon
The Secret Life of Cooper Bennett
He is the Tide
Skyline Memories
After the Ride
Dawn Rises (A Song of Ages Verse 1)
Dusk Falls (A Song of Ages Verse 2)
Strive: Conquest of Stars
Strive: By Way of Starlight
Strive: A Time of Dread

NOVELLAS & SHORT STORIES TO LOOK OUT FOR:
Swole: Wet Wednesday
Swole: Triple Drop Sets
Swole: Flex Friday
Manifest
Stories of the Order – Shadowmen
Stories of the Order – No Strings Attached
Stories of the Order – Mosely

Made in the USA
San Bernardino, CA
08 May 2017